EDITED BY JHORDYNN (318) 406-2249

COVER FORMATTED BY PSALMYY ON FIVERR

PUBLISHED BY MADE 4 THIS™

ISBN-13: 978-1-7365773-5-6

I would like to dedicate this book to my children Carmillo, Kamara, and Kammeyoun. I love you more than words can say, and I wouldn't trade you for anything in this world. I also would like to give a special thanks to my editor/ publisher Jhordynn who was very patient with me and helped me through my journey.

KANDY KANE

BY ARADA L. ARMSTRONG

CHAPTER 1

Kandace wasn't in the mood after seeing her mom the day before. Kandace and her mom were best friends, road dawgs, confidantes… How could she betray Kandace like that? Yesterday evening, Kandace was on Cloud Nine. Her mama made it all come crumbling down.

Yesterday evening, Kandace went to her mom's house like she usually does. The daily routine was that if Kandace's husband Aiden worked in town, she would talk with him for a little while once he got home, then go to her mom's house. If he worked out of town like he usually does, she would go to her mom's house once she was finished cooking and cleaning. Either way, every day, Kandace went and talked with her mom Anna. Yesterday was no different. Kandace couldn't wait to tell her mom to her face that she had decided to go to beauty school like she always dreamed.

Growing up, Kandace and her mom always talked about her being a beautician. When Kandace was a child, Anna bought Kandace numerous mannequin heads, cheap hair from the hair store, and a vast array of combs, brushes, and hair products for Kandace to play with. Anna did whatever she could to make Kandace's dreams come true. But Kandace's life didn't go as planned. She fell in love.

She married her high school sweetheart as soon as they graduated high school, and the children came soon after. There was no time for school, careers, goals, nothing. Her whole life was Aiden and their children: Kaiden, Kase, and Katrina. Kandace never regretted anything. She just wished that she would have taken her time in life and scratched a few things off her bucket list before starting a family. She'd never been outside of Louisiana's limits.

But yesterday, she woke up with a different fire in her. She was back alive. She had put her life on hold at eighteen. Now, at forty-six, she remembered who she was. She no longer defined herself as "Aiden's wife" or "their mom". She was Kandace. And Kandace was going to be a beautician.

She opened her mom's front door with her own personalized key, glided into her living room to tell her that her daughter was going to be a beautician, and was disgusted by what she saw sitting on the couch. She felt the contents of her stomach making its way up to her throat.

"The fuck?" Kandace asked.

"Kandace. It's time to make things right with him. He's your father. While he's alive, make it right."

"Make it right?! Make it right?! I haven't done shit wrong! He hurt *me*! He did *me* wrong! Have you told him to make it right with me?! How the hell you act like I did him something?!"

"I'm sorry, Kandace. The wording was wrong. I was just trying to say that while there's time, give him a chance."

"Fuck him. And fuck you."

Kandace stormed out the house. Her dad, Ernest, ran behind her. "Wait, Kandace! Let's talk!"

"Talk? What do we possibly have to talk about? You did what you did. You said what you said. Now stand on that shit!"

Kandace drove away to the nearest gas station and let the tears flow. That was the most they'd said to each other since she was eighteen. And Kandace was determined that that was the most they'd say to each other to the grave.

Now it was the next day, and her body was heavy. She knew that she couldn't go see her mom this evening when Aiden came home. Her routine was disrupted. What else was there to do on a Friday night?

"Hello?" Kandace answered her phone.

"Open the door, Bitch!"

"I don't wanna," Kandace pouted.

"I didn't ask you all that. Open the door. 'Cause you ain't doing nothing but moping in that house. Open the door!"

"Ugh!" Kandace stomped to the door and let her baby sister in. "Hey, Brooke."

"I'mma let you slide with that dry ass 'hey'. I know your mama done fucked up. But I been trynna tell you 'bot Anna. She ain't right. You were bound to see it sooner or later. She was never a good mama to us. When we get grown and gone, she wants to be mom of the year and shit. When we got our own house and making our own money, she shows up with glitter and lights on. Girl. Anyway."

"That's not how I remember it. I remember her always doing the best she could being a single mother with six kids."

"We'll agree to disagree. But anyways! Get your boring ass out the house and come out with me tonight. Meet me at Club Aye at eleven tonight. I'm working tonight, and I'll make sure you drink whatever you want for free. You ain't got shit to do. I ain't asking you. I'm telling you. Bye!"

"You just came over to boss me around?"

"I'm on my way to eat lunch with your niece. I just had to lay eyes on you."

Brooke sped off on her way to eat lunch with her daughter. Kandace knew that she wasn't going to go to the club. She hadn't been to the club since New Year's Eve 1999. Clubbing wasn't her thing at all. The music was always too loud, people stepping on your toes, bodies bumping into each other, drinks spilling. Plus, she was over forty. Nope! Nope! Nope!

Brooke was eighteen years younger than Kandace. Brooke was what they call "the menopause baby". Anna had her first child at fourteen and her fifth child at twenty-five. Then she had Brooke at forty-three. Kandace was her fifth child, and Brooke was her sixth. Even though there was a gap between them, they were the closest of the siblings.

Kandace always wanted to be a big sister. She had four older siblings always bossing her around. She just wanted a sibling to love. Brooke was the answer to her prayers.

Even though Kandace had her first child Kaiden months after Brooke was born, that didn't stop the love and excitement Kandace had for Brooke. Let Kandace tell it, she had twins: Kaiden and Brooke. She never bought one something without buying the other something. She never took one somewhere without taking the other.

Most people would think that Kandace and Brooke's relationship would be that Kandace was more of a mother figure to Brooke instead of a sister, but it didn't turn out that way.

From the outside looking in, one would think that Brooke was the big sister and Kandace was the little sister trying to keep up. Brooke was full of life, adventurous, fearless, had traveled the world. She was still traveling the world. She had bungee jumped, flown first class. And the thing that Kandace was most proud of: Brooke had gone to college and graduated. Brooke had a Bachelor's in literature. She preferred bartending at the club, but she was most definitely an educated Black woman.

Kandace though to herself, *And who she's calling boring? Just because I'm a housewife doesn't mean I don't have fun. Just last weekend, Aiden and I played Monopoly past one in the morning. But I don't have anything to do tonight. She's right. I'll go. Why not?*

CHAPTER 2

Kandace and her male best friend Shawn met inside the club. He had been trying to get her to go out for over twenty years. She wouldn't dare go out without him. They hugged each other and headed towards the bar for drinks. Brooke had promised her free drinks, and she wanted them.

"Kandace Latrice is out the house? Oh, my God," Shawn sarcastically said.

"Take a picture because this is the last time."

"Anna needs to piss you off more often," he teased.

"The next time she pisses me off, I'mma be in jail instead of the club. Believe that!"

"What are y'all having to drink?" the bartender asked.

"I'm looking for Brooke," Kandace told her.

"What?"

"I'm looking for Brooke!" she yelled. She *hated* clubs for this reason. No one can hear no one.

"Oh! She's up in about twenty minutes or so. We call her Thunder."

"Okay. I'll be back in about twenty minutes. Thank you."

Shawn and Kandy walked upstairs to the second floor just scoping out the place. Kandace didn't know that it was a strip club until she walked through the doors. She wasn't holier than thou or anything. It's just that a warning would have been nice. Of course Shawn didn't mind it at all. He was in his element. He could always bank on a gay man being there with his girl best friend as she celebrated at her bachelorette party. And he was right. He spotted a fine gay man across the room. It was his time to shine. He looked at Kandace, smiled at her, and walked away. Kandace knew what time it was. It was time for Shawn to be Shawn.

She danced to herself a little bit. Mainly, she kept looking towards the bar, waiting on Brooke to start her shift. Brooke promised her a drink or two, and she wanted her drink or two.

As Kandace was looking downstairs towards the bar, someone upstairs caught her eye. He was tall, light-skinned, had locs down his back, muscular, light hazel eyes, and a smile that was bright. He nodded at her. She nodded back. She was embarrassed. *He probably thinks I've been looking at him this whole time. I've been looking for my sister. Oh, my God. And he's walking towards me. God, help!* she thought to herself.

"How you doing tonight, Sexy?" he asked her.

"I'm okay. I'm sorry. I was looking for my sister. She works here. I am so sorry."

"Well, I'm here now. I'm Connor. What's your name?"

She reached out to shake his hand. "Kandace. Nice to meet you."

He grabbed her hand, placed it around his back, and moved in close to her. They were standing chest to chest.

"Don't dismiss me. I ain't going nowhere," he growled in her left ear.

"How many times has that line worked?" she asked him.

He snickered. "It ain't a line. It's a declaration. I'm letting you know that I ain't going nowhere."

"I'm married."

"Congratulations."

Kandace nervously laughed. She didn't know how to react. The only man she had ever been with, thought about, and entertained was her husband Aiden.

"We've been together since I was fifteen," she said.

"Congratulations again. Let's dance."

"I can't. Thank you, though."

"I don't recall asking you anything."

"I—"

Her words were cut off when she noticed a loud thunderous sound. The crowd amped up, surrounded the stage, and the DJ announced, "The wait is over. THUNDAAAAA!"

Kandace looked at the stage and saw Brooke make an appearance like none other. Her outfit was revealing, sexy, just downright breathtaking. Her body was crafted by God. The right amount of dimples, an adequate amount of stretch marks, a perfectly shaped roll. She looked like a woman. A real woman. A woman most women could relate to. She didn't look painted or filtered.

Kandace understood why they called her Thunder. She had no choice but to get attention. Her presence and existence were undeniable. You were going to know she was there.

The way Thunder's body became one with the pole looked like a magic show was taking place. Her body defied gravity. The air obeyed her commands. She walked on the atmosphere. And when her feet hit the ground, she melted into the linoleum. Her body was fluid in every element that it embodied.

"This your first time seeing Thunder?" Connor asked Kandace, breaking her out of her trance.

"Um, yeah. It is." Kandace never took her eyes off of her sister. "She looks like art up there."

"Thunder is definitely a work of art," Connor said.

"She's a masterpiece, no doubt," Kandace whispered underneath her breath, in awe and amazement of her sister.

She never knew that her sister was a stripper. She knew that she worked at the strip club. She always thought that Brooke was a bartender. She was not sure what gave her that idea, but that is what she thought. Maybe Brooke told her that she was a bartender. Maybe Kandy assumed it. Either way, she would have never guessed that Brooke was a stripper.

"You looking at her like you want her," Connor whispered in Kandace's ear.

"Hell no! That's my sister."

"Shiiid. We all Black. That's my sister, too."

"No. Like we have the same mom, same dad, grew up in the same house."

"Oh. My bad. Does that talent run in the family?" Connor asked, moving her hair away from her ear.

"Not at all." Kandace laughed, thinking about how she could barely walk, let alone work a pole.

"I bet it does. You just need someone to bring it out of you."

The applause interrupted Kandace from replying to Connor. Thunder's reign was over, and the crowd hated to see her go.

"When does Thunder come out from the back?" Kandace asked Connor.

"It depends on how many sets she does tonight. I can take you back there to her if you want."

"I came with my best friend Shawn."

"I'll make sure you return to him tonight in a timely manner in one piece."

Kandace hesitated. "How far back do we have to go?"

"Don't do me like that, Kandy. You're safe with me. I wouldn't do nothing to you or let nothing happen to you. I would kill any motherfucker who disrupts a hair on your head. Believe that."

He extended his hand out for Kandace to grab. She grabbed it and walked with him to the back. "It's Kandace, not Kandy," she corrected.

He stopped walking, turned around, looked at her, stared at her in her soul, and said, "I said what the fuck I said, Kandy."

A tingle shot to an unknown part of her nether region. He was so passionate, strong, declarative.

She liked that shit.

"Okay," Kandace replied.

Growing up, her nickname was Kandy Kane. She left that name at eighteen years old. That was a different time, a different headspace, a different set of rules. Now, here this man was, calling her Kandy. As long as he left the "Kane" off, she could roll with it.

They continued walking to the back. Once they reached a purple door, Connor knocked on it. A voice behind the door said, "What's the mission?"

"Mission the what's," Connor answered.

A man opened the door. "Big C. Who you got with you?"

"If I brought her, she's cool. I know you ain't questioning *me* of all people."

"Bet."

Connor and Kandace walked in the room. Purple, royal blue, and gold were everywhere. It was something out of an exotic movie.

"This new to you, Kandy? If I didn't know better, I'd say you didn't know your sister was a stripper."

Kandace said nothing in response.

"Sistaaaa," Brooke sang. "I really didn't think you'd come. Wassup, Mr. Connor? I see you met my heart."

"Yea. Kandy is something else."

"Kandy? Who is Kandy."

"I'm Kandy."

Brooke smirked. Even though Kandy didn't know what was going on, Brooke surely did. Connor was well on his way to showing Kandy a life she never thought of, dreamed of, or even knew about. Brooke always tried to loosen Kandy up, but Kandy wouldn't budge. She was so dead set on being a boring housewife. But that would soon change.

"Okay, Kandy. Let me show you around. Connor, you coming with us?"

"Of course. I own the place."

Connor and Brooke took Kandace on a tour of the strip club. That morning, she woke up *Kandace*. That night, she went to bed *Kandy*.

CHAPTER 3

Kandy never got the free drinks that Brooke promised her. Kandy wasn't a drinker. She just needed an excuse to go back to the strip club. She didn't know what she was looking for or why she wanted to go back. She just knew that her soul was desiring the flashing lights and smoke screens.

This time, she went by herself. Aiden was out of town on business, and the only child that lived with her was at a friend's. It was the perfect night to go out and be grown.

As Kandy was walking towards the entrance, Connor and a beautiful dark-skinned woman were also walking towards the entrance. A lump formed in Kandy's throat. Connor had an effect on her that he wasn't supposed to. Her knees slightly buckled, and her mouth got dry.

"Kandy," he said as soon as he noticed her. "You're back so soon? How did Thunder get you out two nights in a row?"

Kandy had to force the words out of her throat. "She promised me free drinks. I want my drinks."

"I know that's right," the woman said.

"This is my wife Storm. She and I both own the club. She used to be a dancer here. She passed the torch down to Brooke ten years ago." Connor looked at Storm. "This is Kandy, Brooke's sister. Same mom, same dad, same house."

"Great to meet you!" Storm extended her hand to shake Kandy's.

Kandy was a little salty because Connor said nothing about having a wife the previous night. The chemistry between Kandy and Connor was obvious; she really thought they had something. Then she realized that she was married her damn self. She had no room to feel no type of way.

She shook Storm's hand and put on her best fake smile. "Nice to meet you."

"You, too, Kandy. I love Brooke. You said she promised you free drinks. Shit, let's go get them. I had a hell of a day."

Storm and Kandy went to the bar to unwind a little. They drank, danced, laughed, and just enjoyed each other's company. They vibed together as if they had been friends for years. They told each other things they had only told their husbands. They caught each other up on all the years that they had missed out of each other's lives. They even made plans to try the new brunch spot that wasn't too far from Kandy's house the next day.

Kandy was so mesmerized by how free and uninhibited Storm was. She was also a wife and mother like Kandy, but she had her own identity. Kandy loved that Storm did whatever it was that she wanted to do. Kandy wanted the courage and freedom to do the same.

Because they had plans for brunch together for the next morning, Storm spent the night at Kandy's house. Aiden was out of town for the weekend, and Kandy's youngest was spending the weekend with her friend. The house was all theirs. Kandy showed her around the house, where she'll be sleeping, and she went to bed.

In the wee hours of the morning, Kandy felt Aiden's hand stroking her back. It was softer than usual. Not only was the texture of his hand softer, but the weight of his touch was softer as well. He was caressing her, allowing her body language to tell the story. She turned onto her back to allow Aiden access, opened her eyes, and saw that it was Storm making her melt into the sheets.

Storm crawled on top of Kandy, made sure they looked each other in the eyes, and told her, "I want you in every way."

Kandy never knew it until that moment, but she wanted her, too. There was *something* about Storm that intrigued her in every way.

"I've never—"

"I got you," Storm said, cutting her off.

Storm leaned in to kiss her, taking it as slow as Kandy needed her to. Kandy put her hands on the sides of her face, pulling her in to her, letting her know that she had her permission. Storm kissed her with such passion, and Kandy loved it.

"I want to put my tongue between your legs," Storm whispered in her ear.

Kandy's mind hadn't thought that far. She was enjoying the kiss and touch, but maybe *that* was too far. She had never cheated on her husband. She had never been with a woman. She had never been with anyone other than her husband.

"Maybe we should slow down," Kandy suggested.

"Maybe you should relax."

"Maybe I should relax," Kandy whispered. She relaxed her body, and let Storm take control.

Storm moved to her neck, giving her soft, slow pecks. Kandy creamed at the feeling of Storm's warm breath pulsating on her neck. Storm passionately gripped Kandy's breasts and sucked her nipples. Kandy's body seized in Storm's mouth.

Storm proceeded with a trail of kisses and licks down her torso, down her thighs. Storm took her time kissing Kandy's calves to give Kandy ample opportunity to adjust to the thought of being devoured by her. When

Kandy's body said that she was ready to be feasted upon, Storm slowly licked Kandy's clitoris.

She allowed Kandy's body language to dictate the pace. She sped her laps up and interchanged them with making her mouth the letter "O", sucking her clitoris, making Kandy's soul leave her body. Chills went up Kandy's spine. Kandy grinded in Storm's mouth, unable to control her body's movements.

Kandy was always shy in the bedroom, holding in her sounds, but Storm's skills wouldn't allow it. Kandy let out a moan that she couldn't silence. Her body was giving Storm the go, and Storm accepted the invitation. Storm made her tongue as stiff as a board and placed it inside Kandy, going back and forth, in and out, round and round.

Storm looked up at Kandy with Kandy's residue dripping off her chin and said, "I wonder what other hole needs to be satisfied."

Kandy was lost as to what she was talking about. Storm bent her over, made Kandy arch her back, and devoured her ass. Kandy screamed out in ecstasy as her knees gave out. They couldn't hold her body up any longer. Kandy was experiencing pleasure like never before. Storm flipped her back over and put her fingers inside Kandy's pussy while sucking her clit at the same time. Kandy was heated with passion. Her legs were shaking, calling Storm's name, and breathing hard. Kandy's body erupted into Storm's mouth, and Storm drank her juices as if it was the last drink on earth.

* * *

Kandy lay in ecstasy as she replayed everything that happened. She couldn't process it. *How did I end up here? What do I tell my husband? Do I even tell my husband?*

"Whatcha thinking about?" Storm asked Kandy, after she came back from washing her face and brushing her teeth.

"Just... just."

"I used your toothbrush. I hope you don't mind. I saw a pink one and a black one. I assumed the pink one was yours."

"You assumed right."

"What's on your mind? Why you so distant? Did I do something wrong?"

"You did everything right. I'm just trying to process it all. How did all this even happen?"

"Did I make you do anything you didn't want to do?"

"No. You didn't rape me." Kandy giggled. "I just didn't wake up today thinking this would happen. I have never thought about cheating on my husband. Surely never thought about cheating with a woman."

"What you think? Are you grossed out?"

"No," Kandy quickly answered. "Not at all. I just feel guilty that I don't feel guilty about cheating on Aiden."

"You should tell him. He'll want me to join y'all." Storm winked at Kandy.

Kandy covered her mouth in shock.

"Me and Connor do it all the time."

"With men and women?"

"Just with women. He'd die if I brought another man to the bed. But I've been wanting to experiment with another man. Let me know if your husband is down with it. In the meantime, you can practice threesomes with me and Connor. Don't lie and say you've never fantasized about him. I don't mind. You should stop by some time."

Kandy couldn't find her words. She was shocked and flattered at the same time.

"Think about it, okay?" Storm asked her.

Kandy nodded her head in agreement. She had thought about fucking Connor many times. But fucking him with his wife? Never.

CHAPTER 4

"Thank you for coming," Storm told Kandy, as Kandy stood outside their front door.

Kandy was so nervous that she couldn't reply. She walked in the house, saying nothing.

"Kandy," Connor plainly stated. "I got you some wine."

"I made sure we got your favorite," Storm added.

Kandy downed the wine in one gulp. She needed to hurry up while she still had the nerve.

"I'm ready," Kandy blurted out. She had just walked through the door. She never sat down, never took her shoes off, never adjusted her footing. She was ready to do what she'd never done before. What she never imagined she'd ever do. She never imagined she'd wait until she was forty-six to start living outside the box, but there she was.

Taken back a bit by Kandy's forwardness, Connor and Storm hesitated to take her to the room. Her eagerness made them feel she wasn't ready. But when Kandy tied her hair back and got on her knees in front of Storm in their living room, they changed their minds. They had the bedroom set up for a night full of adventure, but what adventure is better than an unplanned one? The living room it was.

Storm grabbed a handful of Kandy's hair as Kandy made progression getting Storm out of her clothes. The heat between the women was visible, and for a second, Connor questioned if he even belonged. If he wasn't invited, he was going to at least enjoy the view.

But fuck that. Connor needed in on it. He needed Kandy. He knew from the first time he laid eyes on her that he had to have her. She piqued his animalistic instinct at first glance. She was a *real* woman. Natural. Put together by God.

Working in the strip club and fucking strippers for all those years made him forget how women really are built. Kandy hadn't had no BBL. Her breasts weren't positioned perfectly underneath her chin. Her thighs and hips were not smooth by any means. Her stomach had not been flat in years, if ever at all.

Her nipples pointed downward. She had a roll or two on her back. Her hips and thighs were dented. Her stomach folded. She was forty-six, and you could tell. She didn't do anything to cover up her gray strands. She birthed three children, which was obvious. Her skin moved with her movements.

And Connor loved all that shit. Truth be told, he wanted Kandy more than he wanted his own wife. His wife looked painted on and put together; Kandy looked like something that was painted by God's paintbrush.

Kandy was on her knees with Storm's left leg over her shoulder, devouring everything that Storm was pouring out.

"Kandy, lay on your back. Storm, sit on her face," Connor instructed. The ladies did as told.

Kandy's pussy was calling out to Connor's tongue, and he answered. He buried his face in her center so deeply that his eyelashes tickled her lower lips. Kandy was trying her best to continue to please Storm as he pleased her, but dammit, it was hard. Kandy couldn't coordinate her licks with his licks. Kandy couldn't pace her breathing. Kandy didn't know how to moan and finger Storm at the same time, but she did her best to figure it all out.

Kandy couldn't hold back any longer. She quickly discovered that the eruption brewing in her lower belly was an orgasm unlike she'd ever experienced. A level of satisfaction that she didn't know existed. The cool sensation between her legs frightened her for a second until she realized she had squirted—something she had never done before. She arched her back and loudly called out Connor's name. Connor licked every drop of Kandy's juices, and he loved it.

Connor climbed on top of Kandy, gently removed Storm from her face, and placed his tongue in Kandy's mouth. Kandy sucked his tongue, enjoying the remnants of herself lingering in his mouth. He looked into Kandy's eyes and inserted his dick in Kandy's soaking wet pussy. Kandy lets out this loud scream, looking up at Connor, not being able to believe that sex felt that good. He saw the magic in her eyes, and it only pushed him to be better and do better.

"How does this feel, Baby? Huh?" he asked Kandy.

Her eyes rolled to the back of her head, and it felt as if she swallowed her tongue. She couldn't answer him. Storm was so turned on by Kandy being pleased that she observed from the sidelines and masturbated to her husband and Kandy's chemistry.

While still rimming his ten-inch hard dick inside Kandy, he lifted her legs and sped up his stroke. Connor could hear Kandy's pussy juices slushing around his tool, and it only turned him on more. He tried to think of something to distract him, but nothing could stop the cum that was brewing. He roared, pulled out of her, and Storm drank his liquid.

"Kandy, you're mine now," Connor declared. He went down her body, kissing her stomach and inner thighs, giving them soft kisses and bites. He watched Kandy twitch and giggle at the sensations. He made a mental note that her inner thighs were her weakness.

He lifted up both of Kandy's legs and spread them apart. He devoured her like she was his last meal on Death Row. She couldn't handle it. She tried to put her legs down, but he wasn't having it. He positioned his weight on her lower stomach to where she couldn't move.

"You're a big girl. You can take it," Storm whispered to her. "Take that shit."

Kandy grabbed the back of Connor's head and grinded with Connor's tongue. She figured if she couldn't escape him, she could control him. And she was right. Her body's movements controlled his tongue all the way until she came down his throat.

"I've seriously had enough. Please stop," Kandy sensually begged.

"Spare her. *This* time," Storm told Connor.

"*This* time," he agreed.

The three of them showered together. Storm took control and cleansed Kandy from her head to her toes. They kissed so passionately that Kandy's body shivered. She wasn't sure if it was an orgasm or just a strong sensation, but whatever it was, she appreciated the experience. The entire night had been a night of firsts for Kandy, and she regretted nothing.

CHAPTER 5

"Why the hell you so damn chipper?!" Shawn asked Kandy.

"I'm always chipper."

"Naw, Bitch. You chipper, *chipper*. Bouncing around here and shit. Your whole demeanor is different. And since when you wear bold colors? Aiden must be putting it down."

"He is," she quickly replied.

"Ooohhhh, you lying!" Shawn jumped up. "Bitch, you lying! Oh, my God. Does Aiden know? Of course he don't know. Your head ain't bashed in."

"Know what?"

"Do you think I'm stupid, dumb, or slow?"

"I hope all three." She grimaced.

"Well, I ain't! Spill the tea. What's his name?"

"Connor."

"Connor?" Shawn distorted his face. "That sounds White as snow."

"He's Puerto Rican and Black."

"Ohhh. Rico Suave. Okayyyy."

"And his wife Sherita."

Shawn dropped his fork. "What about his wife Sherita?"

Kandy went back and forth in her mind with how much she wanted to tell. She hadn't even admitted these things to herself, let alone to anyone else. But there was no time like the present. She planned on taking it all to her grave, but since Shawn was asking, she was telling.

"They both have my heart, but Sherita got my mind. I can't shake her."

Shawn's mouth hit the table. "Bitch. What?"

"Yeah."

"Yeah, what?!"

"We call her Storm."

"That's for shit sure! She done came in, wreaked havoc, and changed the game."

"Facts."

"You always been gay?" Shawn asked Kandy.

"No. Something about her. I can't put my finger on it."

"You putting more than your finger on it." Shawn joked. "Hold up. Have y'all...?"

"Yes," Kandy answered.

"And you...?"

"Yes. Again and again."

"Wait a damn minute! What's up with you and her husband? Does he know? Does she know?"

"Yes. We all know. And we all know that we all know."

"Have y'all... together?"

"Yes."

"All three of y'all?!"

"Yes."

"Oh, my Gawd!"

"I don't know the rules, though. I don't know if it's okay that I sleep with them separately. I want them each separately. The threesome was cool. But I want one on one. I did one on one with Storm. I don't know if Connor is cool with that. If I do one on one with Connor, I don't think Storm would be cool with it. I don't even want to bring it up. They'll get in their feelings. But I'll at least ask Storm if Connor knows that we did it, just us."

"How did this even happen?"

Shawn couldn't wrap his mind around all that Kandy was saying. They had been best friends since elementary. They each knew each other's darkest secrets. There was nothing they didn't know about each other. Until now.

Shawn's feelings were hurt. Did she not trust him with this info? He would never judge her. This was something they were supposed to laugh and ooh and aah about over shots. She was supposed to give him every detail. She was supposed to run the plays with him. But she kept it to herself. How long, he didn't know. But it was long enough to put him in his feelings.

"I honestly don't even know how it all happened, Shawn. I really don't. It all happened so fast. And here I am. My head is spinning."

"And Aiden don't see no change in you? He's not suspicious?"

"He hasn't said anything."

"And that's why yo' ass is cheating now. He never paid enough attention to you. You are obviously a different person than you were a month ago, and he doesn't realize that?! He hasn't said anything?!"

"Don't say it like Aiden is a bad person."

"I never said he was a bad person. But he ain't no good husband. When your hair is different, he says nothing. When you wear a new outfit, he says nothing. When you are glowing, he says nothing. All he does is says nothing! Chile, get it in. I don't blame you. You are a woman. You need acknowledgement, affection, attention. Hell, I'm a gay man, and even I know that. Shit. You went to the people who are giving you what he ain't."

Kandy was quiet for a minute or two. Shawn was right, as always. Aiden never gave her the acknowledgement, affection, or attention that she needed. Yes, she never wanted for anything materialistically. Yes, he always made sure the bills were paid and their children were the freshest dressed kids in school. He even remembered anniversaries and holidays. But *time* and *intimacy* are what he never made his way around to.

"I'm stupid," Kandy said, defeated. "I'm risking my well-being and being a kept woman all for a nut and excitement. I need to go back to watching porn. I got a nut and excitement from that, too."

"Kandace. You *are* risking it all. That is true. But by not doing it, you are sacrificing so much, like your joy, pleasure, happiness. I see what you are saying. But living the rest of your life as a bored trophy ain't it, either. You are still young with decades left in your body. Do with that information as you wish."

Before she could reply, her phone dinged. She read the message and smiled.

"Why are you looking at me like that, Shawn?" Kandy blushed.

"Just wondering if he is grinning on the other side of that phone as much as you."

"I wonder that, too. You were right. Spending the rest of my life as a bored trophy ain't it. Maybe this is my chance to start back dating."

"Whatever happens, I am here for you always. You know that, right? You will always be good whether I'm dead or alive. I got you. For life. I love you, Girl."

Kandy looked at him, smiled, and said, "I love you more."

CHAPTER 6

Sunday morning. Time for church! Kandy's granny always said that there was no mountain too high nor valley too low that we find ourselves in that God can't reach us. She always said that the same way doctors are here for the sick, God is here for the sinners. She always drilled in her descendants' heads that sinning is no reason to pull away from God.

Kandy could hear Granny in her head, "If you pull away from God, how you gonna get back to Him? Your own strength ain't gonna do it. If your own strength could do it, you wouldn't have strayed away in the first place. Even if there's a crack pipe in your mouth, pray to God. He's the only one who can save you."

Long story short, Granny believed in talking to God, no matter what. She instilled that in Kandy. No matter what lasciviousness Kandy was partaking in, she was going to go to church. And that was that.

As she sat beside Aiden in church listening to the preacher, she felt guilty that she didn't feel guilty. She knew that there should have been some ounce of remorse. Something should have been tingling her conscious. A drop of *oh shit* should have been in her spirit, but it wasn't. She literally did not care that she had been cheating on her husband; she couldn't wait to do it again.

She knew God's word better than she knew how to spell her name. She knew that He didn't change just to better suit her. But didn't God want her to be happy? Wasn't He happy that she was finding and discovering herself? Wasn't God rejoicing that she finally was getting the confidence that gave her joy? Surely God didn't want her to live the rest of her life miserable "in Jesus' name". She was over "suffering on earth to rejoice in heaven". Connor and Storm were her heaven on earth. She'd worry about the other heaven when she died.

Sunday's tradition was that Kandy and Aiden go to a buffet after church, walk the calories off at the mall, go home, and watch a movie until the movie watched them. This Sunday, Kandy put on a tighter dress than usual, heels instead of flats, and makeup instead of a bare face. Aiden didn't seem to notice. She wasn't going to say anything at first, but she couldn't hold it in anymore.

"How do I look today?" she asked him at the restaurant.

"Cute," he answered, never breaking his eye contact with his plate.

"You like my dress? It's new."

"Yeah."

"I put on heels instead of wearing my usual flats."

"I was wondering why you did that. Knowing you have that bad left knee. You gonna feel that in the morning." He laughed out loud.

Kandy's feelings were crushed. This was exactly why she didn't feel bad about cheating. That was damn why right there. She excused herself to the bathroom. She sat on the toilet just to get out of her feelings. She needed a second or two to regroup. Once she got herself together, she walked out of the stall.

To her left, she saw a full body mirror. Fuck Aiden. Even if he didn't like what he saw, she did. She gave herself a photoshoot in the bathroom. Multiple body poses. Multiple facial expressions. She even switched her hair up for a few of the pictures.

Girl, you're so silly. You're too old for this. Erase this shit, she said to herself. As she swiped through the pictures to delete them, she decided to send a few of them to Storm and Connor.

GAHDAMN, GIRL! You dress like that for God? Shiiiid. Call me Jehovah Connor texted her in response to her pictures.

Stop playing with me and come here. Let me see how them heels look on my ceiling was Storm's reply to the pictures.

I cant stop lookin at them legs. Turn around and bend over. Lemme see how them legs look from that angle Connor texted.

Don't get quiet on me. You sent them pictures. **Back that shit up. Bring. Dat. Ass. HERE!** Storm demanded.

Where's Connor? Kandy asked Storm.

At the club. He'll be there awhile. This is a me and you situation.

OK. Give me a few hours. Im coming.

 Don't make me come looking for you with a flashlight cuz I will. And leave them heels on Storm ordered.

Yes maam

Kandy took the picture that Connor requested and sent it to him. She returned to the table with Aiden.

"You ready to go?" she asked him.

"Umm, sure. You barely ate anything. You okay?"

"I'm fine. Not hungry. That word that the preacher preached filled me enough."

"Okay. Well, let's go to the mall. It's a pair of shoes that I want."

"Can you go without me? I have to meet Shawn in a little bit."

"On a Sunday? Why would you make plans with him when you know Sunday is our day?"

"He's having a bad day. I have to be there for my friend."

"What time you gotta meet him?"

"Like five minutes ago."

"Where y'all going?"

"I don't know. Just ride, I guess. Haven't put much thought into it. Just being there for my friend."

"What about being there for your husband? This is my only day off. Our only real day we can spend together."

"You don't want to spend time with me. You just don't want to break tradition. You don't even notice me. You've said nothing about the way I look. I've switched it up all the way, and all you said was 'cute'. Any other nigga woulda pumped my head up and let me know that I'm killing the game."

Aiden's eyes met hers with fire. "How the fuck would you know that?"

"How wouldn't I know that? I'm a bad bitch. The whole world tells me, except you."

Where this boldness was coming from, she had no idea, but she loved it and wasn't going to let up.

"If they're telling you that, they just telling you that to fuck you."

"So, I'm ugly to you?"

"No, you're not ugly. I'm just saying people don't give compliments for free."

"So the eighty year old woman who stopped me on my way to the bathroom to tell me how pretty I am wanted to fuck me?"

"Maybe."

"I'll catch an Uber home. Goodbye, Aiden."

"Stop the dramatics, Kandace. Come on, and let's go to the mall."

"If I was being dramatic, this table would be on its side. I'm being a fucking lady."

Kandy threw her napkin down on the table and stomped outside. Aiden sat at the table, trying to not be embarrassed. No, it didn't cause as big of a scene as it could have, but it still was a scene.

He battled in his mind either going outside to get her or letting her live out her tantrum. By the time he decided that the husbandly thing to do was to go get her, she was gone; the Uber was already halfway to Storm's house.

Don't wait up was the text Kandy sent Aiden before blocking him.

CHAPTER 7

"I'm sorry. I know I look rough. I came straight here from the restaurant," Kandy told Storm.

Kandy's awkwardness was back. The rush of boldness and confidence that she had forty-five minutes ago had left her. She was back remembering that she didn't have a porn star's breasts, nor did she have a stripper's ass. She was back remembering who she saw in the mirror: a regular schmegular middle aged mom.

"You look like a batch of fresh laundry. What are you talking about? Turn around so I can see you."

Kandy modeled for Storm the best she knew how. She felt so silly doing it. But Storm had a way of making her feel like she was the only woman in the world. Storm made her feel like no other woman was her competition.

"Is Connor okay with this? Like, are we a secret?" Kandy asked Storm.

"He's perfectly fine. And he's aware. Relax. Don't create drama in your head. *Your* husband is who we're hiding from, not mine."

"I just don't want to cause no drama. I am not a homewrecker."

"Well, I am. Take that off."

Kandy nervously laughed. She had no idea why she was having anxiety. It's not like she hadn't done this before. Storm was no one new. They were past the point of formalities and southern hospitality. But there was a wave of *oh, God* that came over Kandy.

"Don't worry. I have that effect on people," Storm whispered in Kandy's ear, as she slowly undressed her.

Storm was not only a stripper by profession, but a stripper naturally. She knew how to talk to you without saying a word. She knew how to make you cum without touching you. She possessed the ability to make you fall in love with her without ever looking you in your eyes. Her vibe was so strong that it made you question all things common sense and made you do the very things no one could pay you to do. More than knowing how to fuck your body, Storm knew how to fuck your mind.

"You trust me?" Storm whispered into Kandy's ear.

"Yeah," Kandy answered.

"Then lay back, open your eyes, and let go."

Kandy always made love with her eyes closed. But Storm told her to watch her. You didn't go against what Storm said.

Kandy found herself naked on the kitchen table. She didn't remember getting undressed or being undressed. She didn't remember making her way to the kitchen. But there she was. She was along for the ride.

"What's your fantasy?" Storm asked.

"You," Kandy answered.

"What about me?"

"Everything."

"You don't act like it. You be running from me," Storm said, as she rubbed Kandy's clitoris.

"I'm just shy and awkward." Kandy panted.

"Fuck that. Show me I'm your fantasy."

Kandy slid from underneath Storm and mounted her. This was nothing new for them to do, but it felt like the first time for whatever reason. Kandy's whole body was trembling, but she had to keep going. She was the star of the show. She couldn't let the audience down.

Storm moaned in response as Kandy pushed her tongue deeper inside her pussy. Storm spread her legs wide, allowing Kandy full access so that Kandy could take control. Kandy could feel the excitement rushing through Storm's body which only amped her excitement up more. Kandy placed her hand on her throbbing pussy to tame its demands. But her clit wouldn't obey her commands. She had to relieve herself before her desires crippled her.

It was time to show Storm that she was her fantasy. Kandy wanted Storm to be the first everything that she ever thought of. Kandy climbed on top of Storm, figured out body angles, and they started tribbing each other. Electric shock waves traveled through Kandy's core. The soft firmness of Storm's love button drove Kandy wild. She grinded harder and faster, choking Storm with the right amount of grip to make her use the Lord's name in vain.

The orgasm that Kandy experienced from their flesh creating friction blew her mind. She would have never imagined that scissoring would make her body shake in ways that she didn't know was possible. She wanted to go another round, but that nut shut her body down. Even when Storm tried to be the leader, Kandy just couldn't.

"You gotta do some pushups or something if you gonna fuck with me. I don't get tired," Storm joked.

"I'm not tired. I'm done with. There's a difference," Kandy joked back.

Storm laid down next to her, and Kandy put her head on her chest. "Your heartbeat plays my favorite song," Kandy told her.

"Your head is my favorite paper weight," Storm said in return.

"What?" Kandy laughed.

"I don't know. I didn't have anything poetic to say back. But I love you, and I miss you when you're gone. I wish you didn't ever have to leave. I feel my chest cave in every time you take more than one second to text me back. Seeing your car lights when you drive away is the worst horror scene I've ever witnessed.

"Whenever you say 'my husband', my stomach turns flips in disgust because I know I will never have all of you. You will never belong to me. I'm going to have to always share you. That's the boundary with us, and I hate it."

"You say that like you're single. You have a husband, too. You'll never be mine, either. I'm going to have to always share you, too. You come with a boundary just like me."

"Yeah, but Connor easily lets me do my thing. I don't have to hide you or lie about you. We can be in the open with Connor. Your husband ain't going for none of that. I already know. I don't even have to ask."

"He might go for it."

"No, Ma'am. And you know he won't. If you even thought he would, I would have met him by now. You snuck to be here now. I'm not stupid. I know how this goes. I've been here before. And it's okay. I just hate it."

"How many times have you been here before?"

Kandy felt her insecurities creeping back in. No, she didn't think that Storm was a virgin. She didn't think that she was her first. She didn't think that she was the only girl she was with while with Connor. But she was beginning to wonder if she was just another notch in Storm's belt. Just someone else she crossed off the list.

"In my entire life, I have been with four women and six men. You are the fourth. In my entire eleven years of being married, you are the second woman I've been with, and I've been with no other men.

"When I said I've been here before, I meant out of my entire dating life. I had one woman and one man who were married, and I remember what I went through with them. You are the only person outside of my husband I am messing with. I have no desire for anyone else. There is just you. Do you feel the same about me?"

Kandy didn't answer the question.

"Wow," Storm said.

"Until a few weeks ago, Aiden is the only person I'd ever been with. It's like I've opened up Pandora's Box now. I want to know what else is out there. I want to experience more."

"I definitely understand that. No way in hell I could have married the only person I've slept with. But other than your curiosities, am I the only one?"

Again, Kandy didn't answer.

"You don't know if you want me or my husband?" Storm asked.

"I know I prefer you. But I can't say he doesn't run across my mind."

"At least the other person is my husband. I can compete with him. That's fine. He'll share you with me."

"What if he says you and I have to stop the sideline activities?"

"He can't tell me to stop what he doesn't know."

"I thought you said he doesn't mind this. Doesn't he know?"

"Just because he doesn't mind doesn't mean he has to know. No, he doesn't know, and I want to keep it that way. I want you to be my personal secret. I don't need him knowing everything. He may want to join more often if he knows you're here with me, and I'm not with that. I want you to myself as much as possible. He may start asking too many questions about how I feel about you if he knew how often we did this. I just don't need no extra. I just need you. I'm not sneaking with you. I'm just being selective of the information that I share."

"I understand."

"So don't you go telling him, either. Don't mess this up for me and you. I want this forever."

"I won't tell him. You and I want the same thing."

CHAPTER 8

"Thank you for showing up to our sister date. I thought I was going to have to call your assistant and make an appointment with you."

"Brooke, don't do that." Kandy laughed.

"What?! I'm serious. You have been so busy lately. I can't keep up with you."

"I always text you back."

"Yes, text. But sometimes I want to hear your voice. See your face, not through a phone. I want to be able to reach out and touch you. I would ask if you're okay, but you look better than you ever have. Damn. What you got going on?"

"Really?" Kandy blushed. "What you mean?"

"Bitch, you are glowing! And I know ain't no baby in there."

"Can I take your drink orders?" the waitress asked.

"I'll take water with lemon," Kandy said.

"Water with lemon?! You're even drinking bougie. Ma'am, get me an orange soda."

"Yes, Ma'am. I'll bring them right back." The waitress smiled.

"Girl, you are so silly," Kandy told Brooke.

"'Only one thing can make you smile like that. And that's dick. Trust me. I know."

Kandy couldn't help but to blush even more. Words wouldn't even come out of her mouth. "I—I mean—it's not so much as—I mean—"

"Oh, my God. You done got you some new dick. Oh, my God!"

"Keep your voice down!"

"When were you going to tell me?! Why didn't you tell me?!"

"I know *you* didn't, *Ms. Thunder*. All this time, had me thinking that you were a bartender, but you a whole stripper out here!"

"Now, you keep *your* voice down!" Brooke whispered. "I was wondering when you were going to throw that up in my face."

"When you tried to throw the same shit in mine."

"I didn't tell you because I was a little embarrassed. But I wanted you to know. That's why I was always inviting you to the club. I thought if you saw me in action, you'd understand. I figured you seeing it would be better than me telling you. If I would have told you, you could argue me down and tell me I'm crazy and shit. You seeing it would show you that I am made for this. Am I right?"

"Yes, you are."

"And I had been inviting you to come to the club for years. Since I did my second night. I been wanted you to know. But you were going to keep this from me for how long?"

"I don't know. Hell, I'm embarrassed, too."

"Embarrassed of what?! Somebody is actually making you smile?! Shit, we all trying to be like you when we grow up."

"It's not just somebody. It's somebody who ain't my husband. I am out here cheating."

"Girl, bye. Aiden's boring ass deserves to get cheated on. I'm surprised it took you this long to wake up. You 'bout the only somebody who would have put up with that. Girl. Do. You."

"But I'm a Christian. This makes me an adulterer. I'm fornicating. I'm defiling our marital bed. I done got in a soul tie with someone who isn't my husband."

"And that's exactly why I'm not a Christian. Everything that feels good is a sin. Everything that you hate is what is right. You gotta repent for smiling. Gotta ask for forgiveness for laughing. If you think out of line, you're going to hell. If you cough, you have seven years of God being mad at you. I ain't subscribing to that shit. But do you. Be miserable. Hell, you been doing it all these years you been with his ass. What's a few more?"

"Brooke, that is not Christianity. The limits and boundaries are for our safety and protection."

"You have been conditioned to believe that shit. Hell, on the damn plantation, Massa wouldn't teach us to read or let us learn how, but would hand us a book, talking about, 'It's from God.' We couldn't even go visit our family members on the same land, but they made sure we went to church. Girl, bye! But anyway…"

"If people waited until they were married to have sex, there would be no AIDS. If people didn't sin, prisons would be empty. If people didn't lie, there would be no confusion. If people didn't steal, we wouldn't have to spend so much money on security systems. I could go on and on," Kandy said.

"You don't need religion to be a decent human being, Kandace. But I'm not going back and forth with you. Tell me more about Splackavellie."

The waitress returned to their table with their drinks and took their orders.

* * *

"May I have the shrimp alfredo, please?" Brooke ordered.

"Yes, you may. Are the bell peppers in it okay?"

"Hell, yes!"

"Okay." The waitress giggled. "And what will you be having, Ma'am?" she asked Kandy.

"I'll have the parmesan crusted salmon with asparagus and loaded garlic mashed potatoes," Kandy ordered. "Oh! I would also like the white chocolate raspberry cheesecake with caramel and toasted pecans on top. I want that first, please."

"You want the dessert first?" the waitress clarified.

"Yes, Ma'am. Please."

"I'll bring it right out."

"Am I on *Lifestyles of the Rich and Famous*? Where are the cameras?" Brooke began looking around. "Because Bitch! Where they do this at?! Eating crusted shit and dessert first. Our ancestors are proud of you!"

"You are so silly! All I'm doing is eating outside the box."

"Well, let my ass stay in the box. It's too expensive to get out this bitch."

The waitress brought Kandy her cheesecake. "Enjoy."

"Thank you." Kandy directed her attention to Brooke. "Excuse me while I pray to my White God made only for White people."

"Go ahead."

Kandy bowed her head and said her grace. "Want some?"

"I don't know. It may turn me into a snob like you. I'm fine with being a ghetto princess."

"Suit yourself," Kandy said, as she began to eat the cheesecake.

"Soooo the guy who has you smiling from ear to ear name is...?"

Kandy went back and forth in her mind with if she should reveal the name because her sister knew Connor. She knew Storm, too. Connor and Storm were Brooke's bosses. She didn't think it would be smart to say their names, especially because this was something she was sure wouldn't last forever. Especially not between her and Connor.

"I'm not saying no names, but she has awakened a whole new woman in me. I'm not—"

"*She?*"

"Yes. She."

Brooke's face distorted as she stared at Kandy. She didn't know what she wanted to say to her big sister; she was not prepared for that bomb that Kandy dropped. "As in a girl?"

"As in a *woman*."

Brooke began scratching her shoulder out of awkwardness. "Maybe I *will* have a bite of that cheesecake cuz I surely have to think out the box now. Especially since you're eating someone's box," Brooke mumbled. She bit the cheesecake and briefly sat in silence. "Why a girl?"

"Really? It's 2023, and you're asking me that. You're a stripper, and you're acting like I'm outta line?"

"Whoa. Please don't talk like me being a stripper is me being a demon."

"So, me having a girlfriend is me being a demon?"

"Ain't that what your little Bible say?"

"Since when you care about what the Bible says?"

"Since when you don't?!" Brooke's voice was elevated.

Kandy sat back in her chair and folded her arms across her chest. "I thought you'd be happy for me."

"I'm trying to be. You act like this is some normal news. Give me a minute. Damn!"

"I'm happy. What more time do you need?" Kandy asked Brooke.

"Just… just!"

The waitress brought their entrees out. Brooke and Kandy ate their meals in total silence. They didn't even pick up their phones to check texts, emails, or social media. Brooke was in complete shock that a woman outside of her and her mom had Kandy's heart. Kandy was heartbroken that her sister didn't seem happier for her. What was the big damn deal? A woman. And?! Who cares? She was keeping a smile in Kandy's heart. That's all that matters.

"I know you probably have this certain thinking towards female strippers. You probably think that we're all wild, care-free, party animals, and bisexual. I am none of those four. Stripping is just something I'm good at, so why not pay the bills with it?

"I've never been with a woman," Brooke continued. "A woman has never caught my attention like that. I never knew that they caught yours. I've always known you to like men. You always talked about how you love a *man* who smells good. A *man* who takes care of home. A *man* who provides. A *man* who protects. A *man* is who you have always emphasized. Are you bi? Been gay but in denial?"

"I don't know what I am. I don't want to put a label on it. I'm in love with her. That's all I know. When I'm with her, she makes me feel like there's no such thing as gravity. She adores me. Pays attention to me. Like the smallest details of me. If I clear my throat, she can translate it. If I blink for point-one-second too long, she's asking me what's wrong. My laugh makes her laugh. When I smile, that cues her to smile. She's just different. At times, I do wish she were a man. It would make more sense. But it is what it is."

"Fuck it! You like it, I love it. 'Cause Aiden surely never made you smile like this. You have been looking mopey and dry my entire life, and I know it's because of him. You have a glow. Like the damn sun is in your forehead."

"Aiden is not a horrible man."

"Not at all! Aiden is a great man. Just not great for you. He'll be great for somebody, though. Just not you. I am happy for you. I want to meet her and thank her for breathing life in my sister."

"If this lasts long enough, you will. Right now, it's still new. You know how new shit is. It always seems like it's what you've been waiting on."

"Time will definitely tell. If she's the one, I'll plan y'all's baby shower."

Kandy spit out her drink from laughing so hard. "Even if we were man and woman, I'm damn near fifty! And she ain't no spring chicken, either. Ain't no baby, Bihhh!"

"Your situation is a prime example of never say never. Time will tell."

"No, Ma'am." Kandy continued to laugh.

CHAPTER 9

Kandy woke up to thirteen missed calls, eight voicemails, and twenty-seven texts from her mom. Her mom was not a texter at all, so when Kandy saw that her mom had texted her that many times, she shot straight up in the bed. She didn't read any of the texts or listen to the voicemails. She went straight to calling her mother.

"So, you're alive?" her mama said when she answered the phone.

"Yes. Are you okay? I didn't listen to the voicemails or read the texts. I went straight to calling you as soon as I woke up."

"I'm not okay. I haven't heard from you in over a month. And your sister told me y'all went out last night and that you got you a new boo. So, everybody gets to see you and hear from you and enjoy you but me. Enough is enough. This has gone on long enough. I am your mother. You are my daughter. That means it's for life. Come on over here and get you something to eat."

Kandy felt her heart melt and break at the same time. Usually, her mom could make her do anything. But not today. Her mama didn't have the same control over Kandy as she did Kandace.

"No, Ma'am," Kandy boldly said. "Not until you acknowledge what you did."

"Acknowledge what I—Girl, please. I am *your* mother. Not the other way around. I don't have to acknowledge shit."

"And I am an adult who doesn't have to jump just because you snapped your fingers. You hurt me. I made you aware of that. You have known that and have done nothing about it. You have let over a month go by without trying to make sure I am okay from the hurt and damage that you caused. No, thank you. I will not be coming by. And I can cook my own self something to eat. Have a blessed day."

Kandy hung the phone up and started her day. She skimmed over the texts her mom sent her and breezed by the voicemails. They all pretty much said the same thing: Call your mother.

As Kandy was cleaning her house, dancing to nineties music—Bone Thugs-N-Harmony specifically—she heard the front door close. None of her children told her that they were stopping by, her youngest was in class, her husband wasn't getting off for another five hours, and no one had a key to her home. She tiptoed towards the hallway closet to get her loaded Glock when she saw it was Aiden.

"Hey, Bae!" he greeted her.

"Hi," she spoke back, hesitatingly. "Is everything okay? You're supposed to still be at work."

He leaned in to hug and kiss her. She turned her cheek so that he could kiss her face. She couldn't fathom the thought of their lips meeting and their spit swapping. Him touching her waist made her cringe.

"You don't act like you're happy to see me," he acknowledged.

"I'm just shocked. You didn't answer me. Is everything okay?"

"Yes, Sweetheart. I just wanted to surprise you. Spend some time with you. Is that okay?"

Hell no, it wasn't. Once she cleaned the house, she had plans on enjoying her me-time. Nothing in particular. Not even a planned place to go. She just knew that Aiden wasn't in the plan.

"I appreciate that, Aiden. But I made plans for today. Had I known you were coming, I wouldn't have made them."

Yes, she would have. Had she known he was going to come home early, she would have had in-stone plans, and she wouldn't have been home when he arrived.

"Well, I can come with you," he offered.

"No!" She didn't mean to yell that. "I just had a day planned to spend time with myself to get my thoughts and everything together. I'm still trying to process why my mama would have my dad over at her house when she knew I was coming. I just need to spend time with Kandace. I am so sorry you came home early."

He shrugged it off. "That's cool. I can always go to sleep. You cooked anything?"

"There's still pancakes and eggs left from this morning. I'll fix you a plate."

"Thank you." He leaned in and planted a kiss on her lips.

Ugh, she shivered. She fixed his plate, half-ass finished cleaning up, and hurried and got out of the house. *Now I gotta figure out where to go.* Before an idea could come to her, Shawn called her. No matter the time of the day, he was always turnt, amped, and ready for whatever.

"What are we doing tonight, Kandace? It's Friday!"

"We are going to party like it's 1999, Bitch!"

They laughed as they both remembered the last minutes of 1999. It was on the news, internet, everywhere that the world was going to end at midnight January 1, 2000. Y2K was a huge thing that had everybody panicking and in an uproar. Kandy was no exception. All three of her children were young, and she was so worried that they would die as soon as the clock struck midnight without experiencing life.

Shawn had no kids, no nieces, no nephews, no siblings, nothing. He had nobody to be concerned about. He said that if the world was going to end at midnight January 1, 2000, he was going out with a stomach full of liquor and two hands full of dick.

With Kandy worried that her kids wouldn't experience life and Shawn wanting to go out with the ultimate bang, they came up with the bright idea to sneak the kids in the club. In 2023, CPS would be called. In 1999, as long as the kids weren't drinking and drugging, who cared? People minded their own business back then.

To their surprise, they didn't have to sneak the kids in. Kandy wasn't the only person who wanted her kids to experience the club life. When they walked in the club, there were more kids in there than adults. There were so many kids in there that the DJ switched from playing DMX, Cash Money Millionaires, and No Limit Soldiers to playing "If You're Happy and you Know It"; "Head, Shoulders, Knees, and Toes"; "I'm a Little Teapot"; "Five Little Monkeys"; etcetera. The only adult song that played was "1999" by Prince.

The alcohol turned into apple juice. The dance floor turned into a gym. The jigging turned into doing the Hokey Pokey. The gyrating turned into off-rhythm dancing in a circle while holding hands. Instead of people leaving drunk and incoherent, they left feeling like they were thirteen again and didn't have a care in the world. All they wanted was a bed because they didn't have the energy to keep up with a room full of kids, no matter how hard they tried.

The children were in control that night, and the adults learned a lot by allowing the children to lead. They learned how to let go and let everything work itself out. Most of all, that night, the adults learned that when in doubt, dance it out.

When the clock struck midnight January 1, 2000, nothing happened. Nothing shut down. The world didn't blow up. TVs didn't glitch. Nothing. But even if it would have, the adults stopped caring about any of that that around ten p.m. December 31, 1999. And they had the children to thank for that.

"Party like it's 1999? No, Ma'am! I ain't got the same knees from 1999. I shole as hell ain't got the same back from 1999. Shit. Let's just go sit down somewhere and talk about the weather." Shawn laughed.

"How about we get our nails done and get something to eat?"

"Yes! I can sit down for both."

"I'm on my way to you. I'll drive us today," Kandy offered.

"Oh, you're acting new, new. I'm with it. I'll be here."

Low key, Kandy rarely went to Shawn's house because she was jealous of his condo. Not jealous as in she wanted to harm him for it, but jealous as in it was a reflection of everything she didn't have. Every time she stepped foot in his condo, she was reminded of how her life ended at eighteen when she got married and began having children. She oftentimes thought about how much further in life she'd be if she had her own career. How far accomplished she'd be if her house was a two-income household instead of one. She always wondered how far she would have gotten if she pursued her dreams of being a beautician. She knew plenty of beauticians who made six figures a year. She never allowed herself to become one of them.

She loved his condo, but she hated it at the same time. Shawn was a mortgage broker who ranked number one in his division every quarter for the last six years. He was undefeated, untouched, and unfuckable with. He was killing the game, and his lifestyle was proof. Of course she was proud of her best friend. She remembered all of his long nights and early mornings. All of his sacrifices. All of his doubts. All the *all the's* he had to push through and thrive in, in spite of.

It didn't make it any easier on him that he was never in any closet. He was always gay and loud and loud and gay. He always had the mindset that you were going to either love the real him or hate the real him. Either way, you were going to know the real him. He made it to the top being the real him, and she loved him that much more for it.

CHAPTER 10

Aiden worked out of town a lot. Whenever he did work in town, he mainly worked nights. Up until about two months ago, she hated that he worked out of town and overnight. But ever since her life experienced that *storm*, she loved that he was rarely home. Her seventeen-year-old daughter Katrina was the only child left in the house, but she could look after herself. It was nothing for Storm to leave her at the house by herself from time to time.

This night, Storm called Kandy over and told her, "Wear that little thing that I like." That "little thing" that Storm liked was *nothing*. No bra, no socks, no earrings, no lashes, no panties. *Nothing*. Kandy drove to Storm's house barefoot in a coat with *nothing* on underneath. Other than a coat, the only thing Kandy was wearing was a smile.

"Right on time," Storm said, as she greeted Kandy at the door with a kiss. "Come on in. I have a surprise for you."

"Okaayyy."

"Open your mind, okay?"

"Okay," Kandy agreed.

"You trust me?" Storm asked her.

"Yeah, I do."

"Don't forget that, okay?"

"Okay."

"I wouldn't let anything hurt or harm you. I got you," Storm assured her.

"Okay."

Storm blindfolded Kandy, undressed her in the living room, and walked her to the bedroom. Kandy's heart was racing from excitement and nervousness. Which emotion was winning, she wasn't sure. They were both fighting for the throne.

"You told me that you were curious about having sex with other men. I want your curiosity satisfied," Storm whispered into Kandy's ear.

Kandy's heart stopped for a second. Yes, she had said it, but did she really mean it? She had already had sex with Connor. Could she be bold enough to have sex with another man? A man she doesn't know?

Fuck yes.

"I want my curiosity satisfied, too," Kandy whispered.

"I'm Midnight," a thunderous voice said.

The bass in his voice alone sent electrical impulses through Kandy's center.

"I'm Kandy," she introduced herself.

Since she was blindfolded, she had to use her imagination as to what he looked like. She imagined tall, dark skinned, a low-cut fade, and pretty teeth with a gap in the middle. Not being able to see him made it so much more exciting for her.

Midnight laid Kandy down on the bed. The way his breath lingered over her body, she could tell he was going to be a tease. He slowly kissed her neck and growled in her ear. His Rottweiler growl sent chills down her spine.

His hands grabbed both of her breasts. He licked and sucked them into submission. She disintegrated into his arms. She grinded as he slowly moved his tongue down her belly to her inner thighs, kissing and biting. She had had enough of the teasing. She wanted him inside her *bad*. Her pussy was throbbing as if a pulse was between her legs.

His hard tongue touched her clit and massaged it, making Kandy quiver. He erected his tongue like a penis, moved it in and out of her, and got drunk off of her moans. The sensation was so strong that she elevated her hips to alleviate some of the feeling. Midnight put his hands on her waist, pinning her down while he tongue fucked her. She couldn't move. She just had to be a big girl and take it.

"Look at me," he commanded.

She removed the blindfold and looked down at him as he licked and sucked her clit. My God, he was finer than she imagined. He was dark skinned like she thought, but she got everything else wrong. He didn't have a low-cut fade; he had a mohawk. He didn't have a gap between his teeth; he had braces over perfectly aligned teeth. From the view of his arms and legs, he wasn't tall; he was five feet nine inches, max. His eyelashes were so beautiful that they looked like they were extensions. His eyebrows were wild and bushy with lines cut in them. He looked like he yoked people up in the streets on Saturdays and praised the Lord on Sundays.

Got damn, he was fine as fuck.

He put both of her legs back, and his nose trailed its way to her ass. Her legs shook uncontrollably as he ate her ass like an ice cream cone. The feels! She begged him to stop, but she didn't mean it. He knew she didn't mean it. That's why he made it more and more intense.

He stopped, came up, and looked at her. She felt the head of his dick pressed against her pussy.

"You ready?" he asked her.

Before she could answer "yes", she felt his weight inside of her. His dick was huge. She tried to run, but she couldn't. The way he was fucking her had her paralyzed. All she could do was roll her eyes in the back of her head and beg for more. He looked in her eyes to make sure she wanted what she was asking for. The look in her eyes gave him the go. His dick felt so good inside her pussy that her mind couldn't fathom the pleasure. She grabbed the back of his head, moaned in his ear, and demanded him to fuck her harder.

He flipped her over and fucked her from behind. He pushed her head down in the pillow with her ass in the air. She had never felt a dick so deep inside her before. Her knees gave out, and she fell to her stomach. He pulled out of her and ate her pussy and ass, giving her time to recoup.

Mmmmmph, the things this man can do with his mouth, she thought to herself.

Kandy felt his dick go back inside her.

"Your ass and pussy taste so fucking good," he moaned in her ear.

"You ready for me?" Storm asked Kandy.

Storm was standing next to the bed with a strap-on on. Kandy had no idea what was next, but she was down for it.

"Yes," she answered.

Midnight laid on his back, placing Kandy on top of him. He put his dick deep inside her, gently stroking her. Storm pushed Kandy's head into Midnight's chest. Midnight spread Kandy's ass cheeks open and told her to relax. He continued to gently penetrate her while sucking her ear and neck to help her relax.

Storm lubricated Kandy's ass hole until it was dripping down Kandy's and Midnight's thighs. Storm slowly eased her strap-on inside Kandy's ass while gripping Kandy's waist.

"Aaaahhhh!" Kandy squealed out in ecstasy.

"I got you, Mommy," Storm assured her. "Relax a little bit more."

Kandy's weight dropped more onto Midnight who was underneath her, grinding into her. Storm went a little deeper inside Kandy's ass as Kandy relaxed more and more. The more Kandy became comfortable, the more Midnight and Storm sped up.

"Put that ass in the air some more," Storm demanded.

Kandy laid all the way down on Midnight's chest and tooted her ass in the air. Storm grabbed Kandy's waist and plowed into her ass while Midnight fucked the shit out of Kandy's pussy. Midnight placed two of his fingers in Kandy's mouth and told her, "Gag on it." Kandy sucked his fingers as if she was going to get nut out of them.

Kandy creamed and gushed all over Midnight. Kandy screamed out in euphoria uncontrollably.

"You like a dick in your ass and in your pussy, don't you?" Storm asked her as she kept stroking her ass.

"God, yes!" Kandy answered.

"Fuck her ass, Storm. Fuck it! Make her pussy keep coming on this dick," Midnight roared.

Kandy reached behind her and spread her ass cheeks open, helping Storm to give it to her like she like.

"You such a nasty slut, you know that?" Storm moaned.

"Yeah," Kandy agreed.

"Can I fuck you?" Storm asked Kandy.

"Yesssss."

"I said can I fuck you?!"

"Yes!"

Storm slung Kandy off of Midnight onto the bed, placing Kandy on her back. Storm plunged into Kandy's ass while tongue kissing her throat. She kissed Kandy long enough for her to get adjusted to the angle. Once she saw Kandy was comfortable and enjoying every detail, Storm stood up in it and dropped down in it over and over.

"Put that dick in my mouth," Kandy told Midnight.

Midnight slid his dick to Kandy's tonsils. The more she gagged, the more spit covered his dick. Frothy saliva trickled down both sides of Kandy's cheeks, and she loved that shit. She sucked him like she was trying to sip a quarter through a straw. Storm fucked her ass without limitations.

"You want this nut in your mouth or ass?" Midnight asked Kandy.

"Cum in my ass, Daddy," she begged.

He pulled out of Kandy's mouth, Storm pulled out of Kandy's ass, and Midnight placed his dick in Kandy's ass hole. He stroked her, and Kandy instantly grabbed his back. Storm did an excellent job, but ain't nothing like the real thing. The flesh, veins, weight, pulsating of his dick made her cum again and again.

"You like her tight ass?" Storm moaned, asking Midnight.

"Fuck yes. Her ass so fucking tight and wet. Ooh, her ass squeezing this dick."

Storm reached between Kandy's legs and played with her clitoris. She slid her tongue in Kandy's ear to watch her shiver. After Kandy's third nut, Midnight trembled inside of her.

"I don't mean to be the party pooper, but I can't take no more." Kandy giggled. "I have had more sex in these last months than I have had in years. My body ain't built for it."

"It's fine, Ma. I can hold you for a minute. If that's okay with you."

"It's okay with me."

"And you already know I ain't going nowhere," Storm said.

"I know. You live here," Kandy joked.

The three of them dozed off. When Kandy woke up at three in the morning, she noticed that Midnight was gone. She loved having a one-night stand with a fine ass man who she'd never see again. She loved Storm even more for making it happen.

"You leaving?" Storm asked her.

"Yes. I want to be home whenever my daughter wakes up."

"I understand. Call me when you wake up. I'll be waiting."

"I sure will."

Kandy ran into Connor on her way out the door. He smirked and nodded at her. If he didn't know before, he knew then. Storm and Kandy were a thing, and they didn't need his permission to be so.

CHAPTER 11

Kandy's phone ringing woke her up.

"Oh, my God, I'm sorry," Kandy's mother apologized to her over the phone, sounding aggravated.

"Are you really?"

"I said it, didn't I?"

Kandy knew that her mom was never the one to apologize because she never thought that she was ever wrong. So, no matter how she apologized, Kandy knew that she'd better take what she could get because it wouldn't get no better than that.

"Why would you have me come over there knowing that my dad was there? You know how I feel about him. Why set me up like that?"

"Because he has cancer. He is dying. There is nothing else the doctors can do for him. I knew that if I told you over the phone, you wouldn't care. I figured if you saw him, it'd be hard for you to walk away. I was wrong."

All Kandy heard was that he had cancer and that he was dying. Her ears began popping, and her vision was going in and out. She knew that she heard wrong. She just knew it.

"What?" Kandy finally said. "Cancer? Dying? Why didn't you say it that day? You could have said that when I first walked through the door. You could have yelled that as I was walking away. If he's dying, why wait months to tell me? Hell, you could have texted me. You could have been told me! This is some bullshit!"

"You could have not been so stubborn and sat down and talked to him like I asked you to, Little Girl!"

"Don't flip this! You knew something this serious, and you said and did nothing. It's been damn near three months! What if he would have passed before now?"

"He wanted to be the one to tell you, Kandace. I didn't have his permission to tell you. I still don't. But I saw that he is just as stubborn as you. So, I told you because he ain't getting no better. And I thought you'd want to talk to him while he is still in his right mind."

"What kind of cancer?"

"Prostate. You know he never wanted to go to the doctor and get his checkups. He was always talking bad about me getting the mammograms and colonoscopies. I told him he needed to do the same thing—get his checkups. He never listened. Got dammit, he never listened." Anna's voice began cracking up.

Even though Anna and Kandy's dad had been separated for twenty-eight years, she still loved him with everything she had. They never married because Ernest wasn't that type of guy, but they had a real love and a real connection when they were together. When Ernest popped up at her door months ago, that was her first time seeing in almost thirty years, but the fire was still there for him. She wanted him to be the one. He was almost the one. But almost doesn't count.

"Where is he? He's still living at home? Is he in a nursing home?"

"He's still at home. He still lives in the same house. He's not bad enough to go to a nursing home. But he does have a caregiver for a few hours of the day now."

Kandy felt her soul drop a little more when she heard that her dad was no longer able to care for himself independently.

"I'll go visit him. I'm on my way now."

"Okay. I won't tell him because then he'll know that I told you. He's going to say that the only reason you're coming over there is because of his condition. I'll let y'all sort all of that out when you get there."

"Talk to you later, Mama. I love you."

"I love you, too, Kandace."

The ride to her dad's house was the shortest-longest ride ever. She replayed all the happy moments they had before they fell out. She remembered his raspy laugh. God, it had been so long since she heard it. She smiled remembering his limp. Nothing was wrong with his legs. He just thought that walking like that made the women want him more. He wasn't wrong. She could never forget how he danced with two left feet. He couldn't find a rhythm if it had a tracker on it.

She knocked on his door. It had been decades since she was there. She had vowed to never be there ever again. But different times call for different actions. She didn't know how long she would stay, but she knew that she wanted to say goodbye so that she wouldn't regret not doing it.

"Your mama opened her big mouth," he said to Kandy as soon as he opened the door.

"Doesn't matter. I'm here now. Let me in."

He looked around his living room and decided to let her in.

"May I sit down?" she asked him.

"Anything and everything in this house is yours, Kandy Kane. Get comfortable."

"Don't call me that! You lost the right to call me anything outside of Kandace a long time ago."

"You are right. I'm sorry."

The same pictures were on the wall. The same furniture was sitting in the same positions as she remembered. He even had the same TV. Nothing fancy at all was going on. The only thing that was different was him.

He was slim, and that put a lump in Kandy's throat. Ernest had always been a man well over three hundred pounds. Looking at him, she wasn't sure that he was even one hundred fifty. His skin was loose and hanging off of him. It was obvious that he was wasting away.

"How much time they say you have?" she asked him.

"About three more months, I guess. No one really knows. They ain't God. Hell, you ask me, I have until the rest of my life to live. Fuck a timeframe. I am the timeframe. I'm going to live until I die."

She chuckled underneath her breath. He was the same ole Ernest. You couldn't tell him a damn thang.

There were moments of silence and awkwardness. They both hesitated many times to say things, but the words never came out. After the tug of war of words, Kandi broke.

"I'm tired of always having to be the bigger man. I'm sick of always having to make the first move. Being the first to call even though I did nothing wrong. The first to apologize even though I'm offended.

"I'm tired of turning the other cheek, only for people to slap that one, too. I'm done with acting like what people did to me is okay when it's keeping me up at night. I'm sick of letting shit roll off my back even though there's a damn lump in my throat. I'm tired of biting my tongue when I'm crying every damn night from what somebody has done to me.

"I'm pissed that I am here! *You* are the parent. I am *your* child. How have you let damn near thirty years go by and you not talk to me? How have you been okay with that? I would *never* allow that to happen between my child and me. Especially when I know I was the one in the wrong.

"You have never said it, but there's no way you think you were right. No way in hell you think I am to blame. So how, Ernest? *How*?!"

"Because I have been too damn embarrassed! That's how, Kandace! Shit! I have been embarrassed as hell!" Tears ran down his cheek. "You wanna talk about crying every night? Try being a grown ass man in the penitentiary, balled up like a baby in the womb, crying so fucking hard that your shoulders are hitting your ears, and the tears have nothing to do with the crime that you committed or the time you have to serve, but it's from the guilt of the pain that you have caused your child.

"I know all about not sleeping at night. I haven't slept in damn near thirty years. I know I was wrong. No, I don't blame you. Yes, I know it's all on me."

"So why not apologize?!"

"Because I can't!"

"Even though you know what you did was foul? Even though you know it has caused a division between us? Even though it means that you don't have a relationship with your grandchildren? Really?!"

He just sat there, shaking his head.

"Wow. I have nothing to say, Ernest. I really don't."

"Kandace Latrice Hall-Turner. I am so sorry," he whispered, looking down at his shoes. He looked up at Kandy and looked at her in her eyes. "I am sorry."

Kandy waited almost thirty years for that apology. She wanted it so bad ever since she was eighteen. She always imagined that once she got the apology, she would sleep so good at night. That the weight of the world would be off her shoulders. That she would breathe clearer and easier. That she would feel joy on the inside. That everything would come together.

But now that she received it, she felt nothing. It changed nothing. The damage had already been done. All those sleepless nights for nothing. All the years of anger for nothing. All the hate in her heart for damn near thirty years for nothing. All of this was for nothing. She could have moved on with her life decades ago. This was all… for nothing.

"I was just a crackhead in the making, Kandace. Plain and simple. When you on that shit, ain't no logic or reasoning or rationale. All that shit is out the window. So, when I found that twelve thousand dollars you had saved for your wedding, all I could think about was how many hits I would be able to get."

"You didn't *find* that twelve thousand dollars I saved for my wedding. You tore my mama's house up, purposely and intentionally looking for it, and you didn't stop until it was in your hands."

"That was your Aunt Lilah's fault. She did all that talking about how proud of you she was that you saved up twelve thousand dollars. She put your business out there."

"It ain't a crime that Aunt Lilah was bragging about me to my daddy! She's supposed to be able to do that. You were supposed to be happy for me and celebrating me, not plotting on me and stealing from me! Aunt Lilah was not the problem. You were!

"I had to cancel so much stuff for my wedding. It was bad enough that you didn't have the money to throw me a wedding like tradition calls for. But then the money that I worked hard for and saved in order to do what you were supposed to but couldn't, you stole. I went from having a wedding and reception at a venue to getting married in my grandmama's living room. The guests had to eat chili dogs and a dry ass cake that I made. You ruined my day. I didn't even get to have a decent honeymoon. You were my downfall.

"And nobody even knew you were on that shit. You never told us you had a problem. I had to swallow the fact that my daddy stole from me and that he's a crackhead all in the same breath."

"At that time, I had only had one hit. But that high was so powerful that I wanted it again and again and again. I wasn't a crackhead when I stole from you; I just was addicted. But that twelve thousand turned me into one quick.

"I thought that by me telling you that I stole it as soon as I stole it, that would make things better for you. My thinking was that you'd appreciate me for telling you, and that would fix it. Like I said, I was on that shit. It made sense at the time.

"I sobered up in prison and realized what I had done. A wedding is so important to a woman. I don't know what all you had to do to be able to get twelve thousand dollars at eighteen years old, but I know it didn't come easy. Shit, I'm seventy-two years old and still never seen twelve thousand dollars. But no matter what it was for or how much it was, I had no right stealing from you. At all. I am so sorry, Kandace.

"I'm sorry that it took me all these years to say it. I'm sorry that I missed out on your life and your children's lives. I'm sorry that I wasn't the father that you needed me to be. I'm sorry that I wasn't there. I'm sorry that you had to be Brooke's dad because I went ghost. But I'm here now. And I'm going to spend whatever time I have left being a damn good father to you."

Kandace was crying uncontrollably. To hear him acknowledge, recognize, and know that he was wrong and caused damage was the relief that she wanted. Knowing that she wasn't crazy for feeling how she had felt for damn near thirty years was freeing. She still didn't think that not talking to him all those decades was worth it. She just knew that she had a right to feel what she felt.

"I forgive you for all of that, Ernest. But that time can't be made up because your clock is ticking. You are running out of time more than I'd planned. And now I'll have to forgive you for dying. I hate you more now than I ever have."

"I'm sorry about that, too, Sweetheart. I really am. I should have gone to the doctor and got the exams. Life wasn't worth living to me. Now I'm looking at you and wishing that I had done what I was supposed to do. You finna be cheated of a father again. I just couldn't get it right in this life. Maybe you'll benefit from my death more than you benefitted from me being alive."

"Don't talk like that. Please. You're here now. Im going to enjoy your life until you die. Who's to say you're going to die before me? I can go out there and get hit by a car. We all are on borrowed time. Let's just enjoy each other now."

"I can dig that."

Kandy and Ernest spent the rest of the day catching up and going through pictures. Kandy brought him up to date on all of her children, their goals, personalities. He brought her up to date on his wife, kids that he had after Kandy's mom, his business that he was trying to set in motion. They just sat up and laughed and talked shit like they used to do before drugs tore them apart. Kandy didn't know how much longer she had with her dad, but she made a vow to enjoy every moment with him like it was their last.

CHAPTER 12

"I talked to your dad yesterday. And I been meaning to ask you why the hell you told Mama my business about me having a new boo? My business is not yours to tell."

"It just slipped out. She was happy for you, though. And what you talk to Daddy about?"

"Bitch, is you gone let me in your house or not?!"

"You the one who rolled up on my doorstep without saying 'Hey', 'Good morning', 'God bless your day', nothing."

"Hey, Brooke. Good morning, B. God bless your day, Miss Hall. Let me in."

"That's better," Brooke said, as she let Kandy in the house.

"You atheists always want God's blessings without God. How that work?"

"Bitch, sat down and tell me about *your* daddy."

"Can you bless me with some ginger tea, a Frappuccino, iced tea with lemon, something? Where's the southern hospitality?" Kandy asked.

"You Christians always want blessings from us atheists. How that work?"

"Heiffa, run me something to drink!"

"I got water out the tub faucet. No ice. Take it or leave it."

"Hurry up with it. And get your sinks fixed! All that money you making at the club, you can get these sinks fixed. That winter storm was damn near a year ago. Don't make no sense you never fixed them faucets."

"Been broke so long, I forgot it's broke. We been making it just fine," Brooke said.

Brooke brought Kandy a cup of water. Kandy looked at the cup, frowned her nose up, and put the cup aside. She wasn't that thirsty.

"Did you know that Ernest is dying?" Kandy asked Brooke.

"I heard something like that in passing."

"And why you didn't tell me?"

"Like I said, I heard it in passing."

"What's in passing?"

"Mama told me, and I forgot."

"Really, Brooke?! How you forget something like that?"

"Because I don't care about the nigga. He never was there for me, and you know that. I can't tell the difference between him and a can of paint."

"Yeah, he did get ghost when Mama was pregnant with you. He was too embarrassed to show his face because he stole that money from me. Then he became a crackhead. Then he went to prison. So, you're right. You don't know him at all. But you definitely have his personality. No doubt about that."

"You were my mama and my daddy. I ain't stunning that man. But I know y'all had a good relationship until you were eighteen. I'm sorry to hear that he's dying. How much longer he got 'til he kick the bucket?"

"He said about three months, but he really didn't know."

"What kind of cancer?"

"Prostate."

"Damn. Done got his dick."

Kandy couldn't help but to laugh. "You stupid as hell, Bruh."

"Hell. You know the treatment make them not be able to get they dick up. And they pee on theyself after the treatment. I bet that's why he refused the treatment. He probably been knew he had cancer. He didn't want the side effects of the treatment."

"You think so?" Kandy asked her.

"Hell yeah. Prostate cancer is a slow progressing cancer, and it's very treatable. For it to get to that point, he ignored every damn sign and symptom, and he refused treatment. I'm telling you."

Kandy never thought of that, but it sounded very possible. Men and their pride went hand in hand. And men always worried about not being able to get an erection. She knew plenty of men who wouldn't take their blood pressure medication because of the risk of it affecting their erections. She knew men who'd rather risk a heart attack and stroke instead of taking their blood pressure and blood sugar medications. So Ernest refusing treatment because he was worried about not being able to get it up wasn't farfetched.

"Whether that's true or not, we're here now. And I hate it. So much time has passed. We can't get it back. I needed a father. You did, too. You going to go around him now that you know he is on a countdown?"

"Nah. I'm good. I can't miss who I never knew. He never tried to reach out to me. And I heard he got kids after me who he is taking damn good care of. He purposely said fuck me. Fuck him, too."

"I can't blame you. At all. I wish you had better parents. I know Mama wasn't shit, either. I play dumb, but I know she dropped the ball more than too many times."

"Anna shole wasn't shit. But at least she gave me a roof over my head. More than Ernest's ass. But anyway… You gave me a great life. And you didn't fail me. I know you probably think that because I'm a stripper and I don't believe in God that you missed something somewhere. You didn't. You were perfect."

"I know. Ain't shit wrong with me. You just a heathen."

"Facts." Brooke laughed. "How is your new boo?"

Kandy wanted to tell her so bad that her new boo is Storm. She really wanted to tell her about the threesomes they have had. But she knew to keep her mouth shut. Lately, Brooke had become someone Kandy couldn't trust. Kandy hated that, but the truth is the truth.

"New boo is new boo-ing. Everything is better than good."

"And when you gonna divorce Aiden? That chapter is over with. What y'all Christians say? To everything there's a season? That season is bland now. Next!"

"It's not easy to just get a divorce. Especially with us still having a minor child. And I'm not sure I want a divorce. I just wanted a break. This is not going to last between me and her."

"Whether it lasts or not, Aiden ain't it, Kandace. He had your teenage years, all of your twenties, all of your thirties, over half of your forties. Don't let that nigga get your fifties. It's time for you to live. He is a zombie who is draining the life out of you. I have never seen you so radiant and carefree. I like this Kandace. I want her to stick around."

"I like her, too, Baby Sis. I'm just not sure I can take that leap and divorce him. That is so… final. I haven't wrapped my mind around the thought of him not being there. And let's be honest, I cannot afford to be by myself. I start beauty school in two months. It's a nine-month program. Then I have to build up my clientele, pay booth rent, etcetera. I need at least a year and a half before I even think about leaving his ass. Not to mention that I still don't even know how I'm going to pay for beauty school! I just took a leap of faith and enrolled. I have zero dollars!"

"If you decide to really go through with the divorce, you can live with me. I will even get the sinks' faucets fixed."

"Thank you. But I'm not leaving him today. I'm not ready."

"I'm ready! But take your time. I'm here whenever and forever."

"Thank you, Brooksie."

"And I'm sorry about your dad. I wish I could give you those years back."

"I wish you could, too."

CHAPTER 13

Kandy slowly started to rub her clit while sucking his dick. She slid her fingers inside her pussy. She couldn't stifle her moans. The more she fingered herself, the harder she sucked his dick. He grabbed the back of her head, getting a handful of hair, and pushed her head up and down on his rod. His moans turned her on even more. She took her fingers out and tasted herself while looking up at him as he was looking down at her. She slowly climbed on top of him and kissed him. She sat on his dick and went up and down while grabbing her ass with both hands.

"Suck them titties," he growled.

She sucked her breasts which only made him grow harder and harder. He grabbed her ass and bounced her up and down harder and faster. She became wetter and wetter. White cream flowed out of her down his thighs, creating a puddle beneath him. The heat from her became too much to bear. He couldn't fight it anymore. He let out a deep moan, and she knew what that meant.

"You love how I make that dick cum, don't you?"

"Shit, yeah."

Kandy opened her eyes, realizing it was just a dream. She felt guilty for enjoying it so much in her dreams. Even while awake, she could feel and taste him. She wanted to go back to sleep to return to the feeling. God, why did she have to wake up?

Later that night, she went to the club to see Thunder in action. She was so good at what she did that Connor and Storm allowed her to have "One Night Only with Thunder". The whole night would be Thunder dancing, and all the money would go to her. Kandy was so proud of her sister that she and Shawn set aside everything just to be there.

"What are you having to drink?" a familiar voice asked Kandy in her ear.

"A Bombshell," she answered him. "And my friend will have an Amaretto Sour."

"Bombshell for the lady, and an Amaretto Sour for the lady's friend," Connor told the bartender.

"No problem, Boss."

"And make sure they're on the house. They don't get a tab tonight, okay?"

"Got it, Boss."

"Shawn, this is Connor. He and his wife own the place. Connor, this is my best friend Shawn."

"Best friend, huh?" Connor asked, suspiciously.

"I'm as gay as that tie you're wearing. I don't want her. Relax."

Connor laughed. "My tie is gay? Well, my gay son bought it for me, so you may be right."

"So, you're an ally of my people?" Shawn asked Connor.

"I'm an ally of decent human beings. If you're decent, I'm on your team. I know Kandy doesn't hang with just anybody, so I'm sure you're decent."

"Who is Kandy?"

"Me."

Shawn looked at Kandy in amusement. "Well, excuse me, Kandace. I hadn't had the pleasure of meeting Kandy. I'm kind of offended."

"Kandy is the new me who speaks her mind, puts on heels, and wears makeup. You've met her."

"Oh, I love that chick," Shawn said.

"I got a thang for her myself," Connor said.

That's when Shawn realized that he was Connor. *The* Connor. And his wife was *the* wife. He couldn't wait to meet her. He knew the effect that the both of them had on

Kandace. They were the people responsible for turning his best friend from Kandace to Kandy.

"Shawn, I've made sure that Sundae here will take care of you. Order whatever you want. Can I borrow Kandy for a fcw? I'll have her back before the show starts."

"As long as it's okay with Kandace. Kandy, I mean."

"It's okay with me."

"You must try the wings and cheese curds," Connor told Shawn.

"Will do."

Connor walked Kandy to an unknown part of the club. It wasn't as exotic as the champagne room and dressing room, but it still looked better than anything she's ever owned.

"Have a seat," he told her.

She sat down on the plush couch, and he stood in front of her in silence. The silence was so loud that it made her uncomfortable. She stood up to leave, but he placed a hand on her chest, stopping her from leaving.

As she stood there looking at Connor from head to toe, all kinds of sexual thoughts ran through her mind. She wanted him to touch her in more ways than his hand on her chest. She thought about Storm and wondered how she would feel about she and Connor doing whatever was next. After having that dream about Connor earlier, she couldn't help but to follow through with whatever was next.

Kandy felt his dick rub against her thigh. He ran his fingertips up her left arm. His hand went between her thighs, and that's when she knew whatever fight in her she may have had had been diminished. He began rubbing her clitoris and kissing her neck. He slid two fingers inside of her, and she grinded on them as if they were a penis.

He laid her down on the couch, spread her legs as wide as they could go. He continued finger fucking her while staring her in her eyes. She tried her best to keep her eyes open, but the pleasure was so intense that she couldn't. He placed the two fingers inside his mouth and hummed.

"That's why I call you Kandy. You taste just like it."

He left a trail of kisses and licks down her body. When he made it to her inner thighs, he remembered that was her spot. He sucked and licked her inner thighs, sending her into a frenzy. When her body said that she couldn't take anymore, he spread her pussy lips with his tongue and enjoyed his late-night snack. She grabbed the back of his head and grinded on his face to the rhythm of her impulses. She locked her legs around his ears, pushing his face deeper into her love box. She came hard, intoxicating his senses.

He raised up and got on top of her, gently pushing his nine and a half inch dick into her.

"Fuck me harder."

He looked at her and smiled. "My pleasure."

He raised up and pushed her legs back and started pounding her. She moaned louder. Her pussy became wetter and wetter. Connor pulled out of her, turned her over, pushed her head into the couch, pulled her ass up in the air. He teased her entrance with the head of his dick.

"Please put it in. Please!"

He pushed it in her so deep. She couldn't believe how deep it reached. It hit unknown places inside of her. Cum ran down her thighs onto the couch, and neither one of them cared. He pulled both of her arms behind her, locked them at the wrists, and kept pounding her pussy. She came back to back to back.

He noticed that it was almost time for Thunder's appearance on stage. Connor pulled out of Kandy, cleaned them up, and returned her to Shawn in one piece.

"Y'all enjoy the show," Connor told Shawn and Kandy. "I'll be around."

CHAPTER 14

"Babe!" Aiden called out to Kandy. "Um, someone's at the door for you."

Kandy's heart dropped. Aiden knew all of her friends and family. So, for him to say "someone" meant that it was a person from her secret life. Connor, Storm, and Midnight knew not to ever show up at her house. Midnight didn't even know where she lived. What the fuck?

Kandy turned the corner slowly, thinking of a lie to tell Aiden. There was a young lady standing in the doorway. She looked to be no more than twenty. Kandy had never seen her before in her life.

"Hi?" Kandy greeted her.

"Hi. I'm Charna."

"I'm Kandy."

Charna had a nice sized locked wooden box in her arms. She was trembling a little, making the box tremble with her.

Charna exhaled. "I know all about you. I am Ernest's daughter."

Unknowingly, Kandy exhaled. She had always known there were other siblings, but it never crossed her mind to meet them. She wasn't prepared to be face to face with one of them. She self-consciously began fixing her hair and straightening her clothes. She felt as though she should have looked better for the situation.

"Hi, Charna. Come on in."

"No, thank you. I am in a rush." Charna looked behind her. "My mom is waiting on me. When Daddy was first told that he had cancer, he told me that whenever he passed, make sure you got this box and its key. I don't know what's in it. But Daddy passed this morning, and I'm honoring his wish." Charna handed Kandy the box and key. "You know he didn't do nothing legal, so there's no will or anything. And he had already picked out his casket and suit. One of my siblings will let you know the details of the funeral once we get them. Have a great day."

Charna wiped her tears and walked to her mom's car. They drove off, leaving Kandy there standing there holding a box, a key, and a face full of tears.

"Kandace. Come on in, Baby," Aiden told Kandy, gently pulling her into the house.

Her body couldn't move. It was frozen solid.

"How could he?" she whispered. "How dare he die?"

"Come on in, Sweetie. We'll talk about it in the house."

"He really did this to me!" Kandy was screaming, and she couldn't stop. "That bastard! That son of a bitch! Just when he started back coming around! Just when I forgave him! Just when I let him back in! Why would he do this to me?! I hate him! I hate him, I hate him, I hate him!"

Aiden picked Kandy up and walked her into the house. He sat her on the couch and removed the box and key out of her hand.

"At least y'all made it right between y'all before he died. A lot of people aren't blessed enough to be able to do that. I am so sorry, Baby. So sorry."

Kandy fell into Aiden's chest and let the tears pour. She cried herself to sleep. When she woke up, she realized that Aiden had put a blanket over her and a pillow under her head. She was so lightheaded. She still couldn't process that her daddy was dead. She saw that she had missed notifications from her mama and Brooke offering their condolences. She couldn't return their notifications just yet. She needed time alone with herself and this box.

She stared at it, trying to figure out what could be in it. After racking her brain for about thirty minutes, she came to the conclusion that it was her grandmother's— Ernest's mother's—recipes. Grandma Ruby could cook like no other. She had all of her recipes scattered around the house. No one knew where they were located when she was alive.

When she died, Ernest found some in the attic, basement, underneath sinks, in fans, under mattresses. Ernest put them all together, and Kandy never saw them after that. She always asked for them, but Ernest would always say, 'You'll have to pry these recipes out of my cold, dead hands.' Well, he was almost right. He gave them to her as soon as he died.

I'm finally going to get that teacake recipe! Kandy said to herself.

She opened the box and screamed. The box was full of one hundred dollar bills. They were packed jam tight in the box. There was a handwritten letter on top.

My Kandy Kane, how can I make this up to you? What have I done? I am sitting here on my prison cot feeling like the world's sorriest father. It is May 9, 2003. Four years ago, I stole twelve thousand dollars from you. I was chasing a cocaine high. Plain and simple.

I wish I could tell you that I stole it so that I could get some kind of medical treatment or to buy a house or a car. But the truth is I was chasing a high. I am sober now, and I can think clearer than I ever could. I doubt you'll get this letter while I'm alive. I don't have the balls to apologize or admit my wrongs.

But starting two years ago when I got locked up, I started selling drugs and cigarettes in here. My goal?

To give you your money back plus some. I made your twelve thousand dollars back, and I will add two thousand dollars every year until I die. As of now, I've made you fourteen thousand dollars.

I pray I die before you so you can enjoy it. I pray you have a good amount of years left alive when you get it so that you can do something with this. I know I can never make it up to you. Please accept this as a piss poor apology. Maybe by now, you're a beautician, and you can use this money to upgrade your shop. Or maybe you want to go back to college, and this can pay for some books. Or maybe you never went to beauty school, and this can pay for it.

Or hell, maybe this can pay for your divorce. No offense, but Aiden ain't for you. And if you're still with him when I die, well... maybe this money will help change that.

Shit, maybe you can blow this shit. You deserve it. You've earned it. You owe no one an explanation. Have at it, my Kandy Kane. Enjoy yourself.

Kandy frantically counted the money. Fifty-two thousand dollars was in that box. And her grandmother's recipes were underneath the money, with the teacakes recipe being on top. She couldn't catch her breath. She had such conflicting emotions: sadness and joy, sorrow and happiness, pity and excitement. She almost used a hundred dollar bill to wipe her tears.

She hurriedly put the money back in the box. She placed the recipes on top just in case someone found the box and tried to be nosey. They would think that it was just recipes and would put it back. No one in her house cooked. She was the only one.

She wasn't going to tell a soul about the money. There was no one she could trust. Whenever Aiden would ask her what was in the box, she would tell him recipes, and she would show him a few to back it up. First thing in the morning, she was going to open a bank account outside of their joint account and would deposit the money in her own account.

When she made the decision to go to beauty school in a few months, she had no idea how she would pay for it. She just stepped out on faith that it would happen. This is how it would happen. She was ready for the new chapter in her life. It was time. She couldn't stay stuck any longer.

CHAPTER 15

Kandy went back and forth in her mind as to if she would attend Ernest's funeral. She wanted to remember him alive. She didn't want the last time she saw him to be him lying on his back, face up to the ceiling of a church. But she felt that she would feel a sense of guilt for not going. Especially after he left her fifty-two thousand dollars cash. That's the least she could do—go to his funeral and tell him goodbye.

Fifty-two thousand dollars may not seem like much to a lot of people. But Ernest was poor. He didn't have a life insurance policy. He owned nothing. He was behind on house payments. He didn't even have a vehicle. Kandy knew that fifty-two thousand dollars to him was like fifty-two million dollars to others.

"Good evening, Church. I'm Pastor Claiban. I was Ernest's pastor in prison. I baptized him while he was serving his sentence. We kept in touch once he was free. I loved him like a brother.

"When he was told he was dying, he gave me this letter to read at his funeral. Now, we are in church, so I have to edit the language. But y'all can fill in the blanks."

The congregation laughed. Everybody knew Ernest. He said what he wanted to say, and he didn't care how it was taken.

"He said he didn't want no eulogy because he didn't want nobody lying on him—his words, not mine. He just wanted this letter read. He said after this letter is read, sing 'My Way' by Frank Sinatra, drop his body in the ground, and go eat.

"Here's the letter that Ernest himself wrote: 'He loved everybody.' Yes, I loved everybody to leave me the hell alone. 'He prayed for his enemies.' Yes, I prayed that God would give them debilitating strokes that brought them two centimeters from death, and they would have to live the rest of their lives in a nursing home realizing they are in this predicament because they effed with me. 'He helped the homeless.' Yes, I helped the homeless get out of my face begging me for ish. 'He kept the unfortunate.' Yes, I kept them in my thoughts and prayers. 'He attended church faithfully.' Yes, I went to church every Sunday and Wednesday for a year because the deacon owed me money. 'He paid his tithes and offering.' I sure did because I found out I could write that off on my taxes.

"This is me. Ernest Wayne Jeter. I had three sets of children, and I never married any of their mothers. I served ten years in prison for robbery. I should have served a lifetime for abandoning my children. They should have never let me see the light of day for how I treated their mothers.

"I found Jesus laying on my back, looking up in my cell. But I never allowed Him to humble me enough to make all my wrongs right. My prayer is that my children are blessed by my death because my life cursed them. I wasn't any good to any of them. I was better to some of them than the others, but I still wasn't ish.

"Let's not get me started on me being a friend. I barely know how to spell it, let alone be one. I've had many friends, but I wasn't a friend to many. I wasn't a friend to myself, so please don't be offended if I was a crappy friend to you. Let me be the proof that you can't expect love from someone who doesn't love theirself. When someone is their own enemy, they can't be no good to you.

"I stole from my mama and lied to her, even on her death bed. I killed my dad when I was twelve. They say it was because he was beating my mama. It was actually because he wouldn't give me money to buy a soda. My mama knew that was the truth. Even though I was always lying to her and stealing from her, she kept that secret between us until her grave.

"I was a no count brother. I never fought my sisters' boyfriends when they got out of line with them. I never lied for my brothers. I wasn't a ride or die. I didn't stick beside them for anything.

"My whole life, I've been all about me. Only me. Whatever benefitted me. Whatever would advance me. Whatever would promote me. Even if that meant stepping on somebody else and betraying someone else to get there.

"I don't know if I'm going to heaven. And Satan is too afraid I'll do his job better than him, so I doubt I'm going to hell. I don't believe in purgatory. Ain't no way I'mma be reincarnated as a butterfly. I don't know what's going to happen once I close my eyes for good. I just know that I sucked at life. So, don't cry for me. The world is better now that I'm gone. Please dance, party, drink, smoke—whatever your poison is. Don't stop life because of me. Until next time, Ernest."

The choir sang "My Way" by Frank Sinatra. Tears streamed down Kandy's face as she listened to the lyrics. She knew every lyric, the composer, where the song was recorded, what Frank wore when he recorded it. That was Ernest's favorite song, and he played it every day, all day.

He had that song on an 8-track, cassette tape, vinyl, and CD. If he downloaded it, Kandy didn't know because she didn't communicate with him during the new age times. But that was definitely his favorite song, and the lyrics were the soundtrack to his life. So, if he downloaded anything, he downloaded that song.

Kandy went to the gravesite. She shook hands with people she hadn't seen in a while. She met siblings she didn't even know she had. When it was time to go, she placed a white rose on his casket and whispered to his aura, "The record shows you took the blows and did it your way."

CHAPTER 16

"I am so happy to see you, Kandy. I thought you'd never come up for air again," Storm told her.

"It was just a lot to take in. Eighteen years of him being my best friend. Thirty years of not talking to him. Two weeks of talking to him. He dies. That's the timeline. That's the end of the story. Close the book."

Kandy was laying on Storm's chest. They were fully clothed. The only part of Kandy's body that Storm touched was her back. She rubbed it and caressed it over and over to try to soothe her as much as possible.

"I hate that. You were cheated. I get it. I am so sorry, Kandy."

"I'm healing. And I'm trying to look at it from the angle that a lot of people don't even get the amount of time with their dads that I did. There's someone out there willing to trade places with me. I know that it could get worse. I know that I don't have the saddest story."

"But don't minimize your pain in honor of someone else. Feel what you feel. See it how you wanna see it. This is your life. Your daddy. Your emotions. It is what it is.

Don't go comparing your situation to someone else's. Whatever your truth is, feel it. No apologies."

"You are so right. Thank you. And thank you for last night. The homecooked meal, candlelit room, full body massage by Nicholas, low playing music… thank you. I needed all of that. I don't even remember going to sleep."

"I know you needed it because you were snoring like a Braham bull."

'Shut up!" Kandy laughed. "Give me mercy. I been through a lot. My life is totally different than it was a few months ago."

"I'm giving you all the mercy, Babe. I don't even care that you talking to me with your morning breath burning off my eyebrows."

"Oh, my gosh! Let me go. I will *not* be the subject of your roasting session." Kandy joked as she got dressed. "I gotta go home anyway. I got some loose ends I need to tie up."

"You're coming back later, right? Connor won't be back 'til next week. And your daughter is spending all spring break with your mom. You don't have an excuse to not come back."

Kandy leaned down and kissed Storm. "Yes, I'm coming back. Have that thang ready for me."

"I sure will." Storm blushed.

When Kandy walked in her house, it was eerily quiet. So eerie that she almost turned around and drove off. She walked into her room, and saw her husband in the bed, under the covers. He had pillows on top of the covers next to him.

"Hey, Sweetie," she spoke, as she leaned in for a kiss.

"Hey," he spoke back, voice trembling.

"How was your day?"

"I don't feel good. Can you go to the store and get me something for my stomach?" Aiden asked her.

"I sure will. Brooke, you want to come with me?" Kandy pulled the covers off Aiden, revealing Brooke in the bed with him.

Brooke and Aiden both looked like deer caught in headlights.

"You thought I didn't know?" Kandy directed towards Brooke. "All that 'Kandace, you need to leave him. He doesn't deserve you. He doesn't bring out the best in you.' Blah, blah, blah. Bitch, I ain't stupid. And all that encouraging me to cheat and stay away from my husband. It took me a while to put it together, but I did. And that's why I put super glue in the KY Jelly."

"Bitch, you did what?! I'mma kill you!"

"Do it now. Oh, you can't, can you? You're stuck, ain't ya?"

"Kandace." Aiden helplessly breathed her name. "Please fix this."

"You want me to unstick y'all when the only reason you're stuck is because you were cheating on me with my own sister?! Why the fuck would I do that?"

"Kandace, please." Brooke begged. "I am so sorry."

"You're only sorry that you got caught. Y'all been doing this too damn long. You ain't sorry!"

"How did you even know?" Aiden asked her.

"When I noticed how Brooke was always encouraging me to leave you, that made me suspicious. Then I noticed KY in your backpack. That bitch ain't been able to get wet on her own ever since she had a hysterectomy. You shole as hell don't have to use it on me. Then I been watching the cameras that you didn't know I put in the house."

"What?! You did what?!"

"So don't even lie and act like this was the first time. I been watching y'all for months! So fucking disrespectful! In *my* house?! In *my* bed?! On *my* couch?! On *my* kitchen counter? On *my* dining room table?! On *my* wall in *my* office?! Since y'all can't be without each other, y'all are *stuck* together now. Have a blessed day."

"Kandace!" Aiden yelled, as she was walking away.

She turned around and said, "It's Kandy, Bitch!" and continued to walk to her car.

THANK YOU FOR READING! PLEASE LEAVE A
REVIEW WHEREVER REVIEWS ARE ACCEPTED!

.

www.ingramcontent.com/pod-product-compliance
Lightning Source LLC
Chambersburg PA
CBHW060428260626
47161CB00005B/1839